Hermie
the
Hermit Crab

by Jo Schmidt
illustrated by Anne Sulzer

D0095983

Table of Contents

Chapter I
A Cradle for Crabs

My name is Hermie. My mother was a land hermit crab. She laid her eggs on the wet rocks next to the sea.

When I hatched, I floated in the warm ocean. I saw many other baby hermit crabs there. That is where I met my friend Harriet.

As we grew, we molted. We slipped out of the hard skin around our body.

When we had molted for the last time, we knew it was time to swim to shore.

Our lungs were changing. Soon we would only be able to breathe air.

"Let's leave the ocean together, Hermie," said my friend Harriet.

We were excited about what life would be like on land.

Chapter 2
A Home for Hermits

The closer we swam to shore, the warmer the water felt. Up, up, up, we swam. Then we breathed air for the first time! The waves pushed us onto the shore.

"I'm faster than you!" yelled Harriet.

We needed to find somewhere cool and safe to rest. The sand was too hot. Hungry seabirds fluttered nearby.

We crawled into wet, cool seaweed. It was a perfect place to hide. It was good to eat, too!

We found a lot of other things to eat, like sea sponges and pieces of driftwood.

"We can't stay here!" I cried. "We need to find some shells that will keep us safe. Let's look in that rock pool."

"Found one," called Harriet, as she vanished inside an old pipe.

She soon recognized that the pipe wasn't a good home. It was too heavy!

Then we found a lot of empty sea snail shells. They were just right.

I snuggled my soft body inside of one. I left my legs and large claw outside.

Then Harriet found her shell. Now we felt safe on the shore!

Chapter 3
Beach Party

It was fun living on the beach. Mostly we came out at night.

We enjoyed being together. We were like one great big family. We would swap shells and claw wrestle.

I liked crawling on the beach in the early morning. During the day we found new places to hide from the hot sun.

Chapter 4
New Homes

My body had grown again and my skin felt tight. I needed to molt. I dug into the wet sand, digging deeper and deeper.

And that is where I stayed until my new skin hardened.

When I came out of the sand, I needed to find a bigger shell. But first I went to find Harriet.

Then I saw the shell I'd last seen her wear. I peered inside, but Harriet wasn't there.

So I tried on that shell. It fit!

"Who's wearing my old shell?"
a voice giggled.

"Harriet!" I cried. There was Harriet
in a new shell.

"Come on, Hermie," said Harriet.
"I've found a great new place. I'm a faster swimmer and a faster climber!"

Harriet was climbing a tree!

I climbed the tree with Harriet and rested in its shade.

We were happy in our new homes.

Comprehension Check

Retell the Story

Use an Inference Chart and the pictures to help you retell this story.

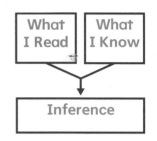

Think and Compare

1. Turn to page 7. What does Hermie need to make himself safer as he grows? *(Make Inferences)*

2. In what place nearest to your home might you see hermit crabs? *(Apply)*

3. How is the crabs' shelter like the shelter people need? *(Analyze)*